D1243548

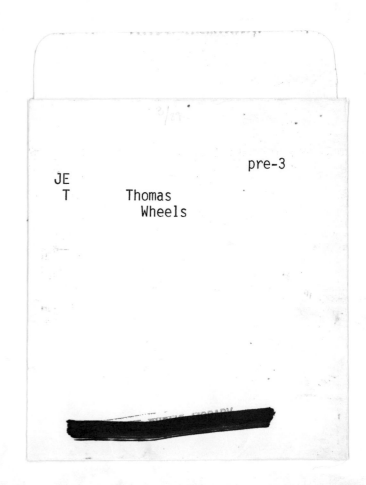

JE
T   Thomas   pre-3
             Wheels

WHEELS

By Jane Resh Thomas
Pictures by Emily Arnold McCully

Clarion Books
TICKNOR & FIELDS: A HOUGHTON MIFFLIN COMPANY
New York

Clarion Books
Ticknor & Fields, a Houghton Mifflin Company

Library of Congress Cataloging-in-Publication Data
Thomas, Jane Resh.
Wheels.
Summary: Five-year-old Elliot learns that winning
isn't everything when he begins to race with the Big
Wheel bike he got for his birthday.
[1. Bicycles and bicycling—Fiction] I. McCully,
Emily Arnold, ill.   II. Title.
PZ7.T36695Wh 1986   [E]   85-13291
ISBN 0-89919-410-9

Y 10 9 8 7 6 5 4 3 2 1

For Elliot Baker Schiffer and Kai Munson Benson

Elliot's birthday present, the one from Grandpa, was
big enough. Elliot held his breath as he tore the
butcher paper off.

There were the red handlebars he had wished for, the pedals, the big black-and-silver wheel. Now he could join the races at the park, instead of just watching.

"Get your bike, Jim," called Elliot to his friend from next door. "I want to try my new one out."

They left the other presents unopened, beside the cake with its five snuffed candles. The whole family came out on the sidewalk.

"Don't cross the street," said Mom as the riders started off.

"Watch out for Sadie," said Dad.

"Go to it, Wheels!" shouted Grandpa. "Feel the wind in your hair."

"Hey, Wheels," called Mr. Palladini, who was loung-
ing on his steps in the last of the evening sun. "Happy
birthday!"

Elliot and Jim drove lickety-split to the end of the block. They swerved around the big maple tree that grew near the curb. They swung around the red fireplug.

Mrs. Morton's old dog, Sadie, heard the clatter of their wheels and limped across the sidewalk to safety. She watched them from Mrs. Morton's top step.

Up and down the block they rode, back and forth past their houses. When it was too dark to ride any more, they started the birthday party again. Mom lit five new candles, and Elliot opened the rest of his presents.

After everyone had gone to bed, he lay awake, thinking about the Saturday races. He would beat everybody, even Jimmy. He fell asleep with his bike beside his bed, his hand on its big yellow seat.

All the next week, Elliot and Jim practiced for the race. On Saturday morning, Grandpa took them to the starting line by the wading pool. Three other boys were there, and Katy from across the street.

Elliot thought about the prize he would win, a big red number one to pin on his shirt. He felt his heart pounding. "I'm going to beat you, Jimmy," he said. "I'm going to beat everybody!"

The other boys laughed. "Listen to the little shrimp brag," said the biggest one.

"Ready!" called the park director.

Elliot got ready.

"Set!"

Elliot shifted in his seat.

"Go!"

Elliot heard Grandpa yell above the din. "Go, Wheels! Go, Jimmy!"

Elliot pedaled as hard as he could. He and Jimmy
stayed even. But by the time they rounded the curve
by the jungle gym, the three other boys and Katy were
far ahead. Elliot could taste their dust in his mouth.

Grandpa was waiting by the pool when the biggest
boy came in first.
Katy finished second.
Elliot and Jim tied for last place.

"I'm proud of you for trying hard right to the end," said Grandpa.

"We lost," said Elliot.

"Winning isn't everything," said Grandpa.

"It is to me," said Elliot. Without waiting for the prizes, he left his bike beside the pool and headed for home. Grandpa picked up the bike.

Jim rode home beside Grandpa, but Elliot got there first.

Elliot stayed in his room the rest of the morning.
He sat on the steps in the afternoon.
Jim came over with a smudge of peanut butter on his chin. "Do you want to play marbles, Elliot?"
"No."

"Do you want to play robots?"

"No."

So Jim rode his bike up and down, back and forth, alone. Elliot stepped on ants.

After a while, Grandpa came out and sat down beside Elliot. He said, "Ants like the sunshine too, you know."

They watched Jimmy swerve around the maple tree, around the fireplug. Jim was riding so slowly that Sadie stayed stretched out on the sidewalk.

Up the block, Katy's mother brought her across the street, carrying her pink-and-blue bike. Jim waited for her to catch up, and they sped away together. Little stones spun out from under their wheels.

"I made a prize for you," said Grandpa. "It says WINNER, because everyone who tries something wins in here." He tapped his chest.

Elliot pinned his prize on his shirt.

Jimmy and Katy sped by the house, howling like fire engines. Elliot imagined himself roaring down the street with them, the siren screaming in his throat.

"Maybe I can catch them," he said.

"I wouldn't be surprised," said Grandpa.

As Elliot climbed aboard his bike again, he and Grandpa waved each other a kiss. Then Elliot sped away to catch his friends. Little stones spun out from under his wheels, too.

Sadie limped across the sidewalk and climbed to safety at the top of the steps.

"Go, Wheels!" called Grandpa. "Feel the wind in your hair!"